Peter and the Wolf

a traditional tale
retold by Nicola Baxter

illustrated by Cliff Wright

IN A COTTAGE NEAR
A DEEP, DARK FOREST,
A BOY CALLED PETER LIVED WITH
HIS GRANDFATHER.

Between the cottage and the forest, there was
a grassy meadow. It was a beautiful place,
especially when the sunshine sparkled on the
water in the cool, still pond.

But the meadow was a forbidden place.
Grandfather had warned Peter never
to go there alone. "There's a
hungry wolf in the forest.
And he might come out
and eat you."

But Peter wasn't so sure. He had never seen the wolf and he certainly wasn't afraid.

So early one morning, when dewdrops still glittered on the grass, Peter opened the garden gate and went into the meadow.

Swish! Swash! He walked on and on through the long, green grass.

A little bird chirped, high
up in a tree.

"Hello, Bird," called Peter.
"Have you seen the
wolf today?"

"No, no, no,"
sang the bird,
shaking her feathers.
"But I can see a plump,
white duck. The wolf
would like to eat her.
He is *always* hungry."

Peter looked round. Grandfather's duck had followed him out of the garden.

"I'm so glad you left the gate open," she quacked at Peter. Then she waddled over to the pond. She wanted to dabble her feet in the cool, still water.

Peter walked on across the meadow. "I hope Grandfather doesn't notice," he thought. "He always tells me to shut the gate."

Over by the pond, the bird and the duck
had started to quarrel over who was the best.

"But you can't fly!" screeched the bird.

"I can!" squawked the duck.
"I just don't that's all. You can't swim!"

"I just don't that's all,"
twittered the bird, and she ruffled her
feathers angrily in reply.

Peter laughed and stopped to watch them.
Just then he spotted a twitching tail.
A cat was creeping through the grass.
But the bird and the duck were much too
busy squabbling to notice. The cat narrowed
her yellow eyes…

and got ready to pounce!

"Look out!"

called Peter.

The cat sprang and the
bird fluttered up into
a tree, just in time.

"Thank you!" chirped the bird to Peter!

Peter laughed, the bird sang, and the duck quacked happily.

But Grandfather had seen the open gate and he stomped angrily into the meadow.

"Do you want to be dinner for the hungry wolf?" he shouted to Peter. "Come straight home!"

So Peter did as he was told and went back, followed by the bird and the cat.

Grandfather said nothing. He stood at the gate until Peter was safely back in the garden.

Then he closed the catch and went indoors.

No one noticed the duck still swimming in the pond. She dipped and dived in the water, and preened her feathers. She would be much happier here than in Grandfather's garden.

But she hadn't seen the hungry wolf prowling at the edge of the forest. He had heard raised voices and come out through the trees.

His eyes gleamed brightly as he scanned the meadow. Then he noticed the plump, white duck. He bounded over, splashing through the water, and caught her. Then…

Gulp!

He swallowed her whole…

And he was still hungry.

Not far from Grandfather's cottage, the cat and the bird sensed danger. They fled to the safety of the tree top and spotted the wolf. They were so worried that they forgot to be bothered by each other.

They watched the wolf getting closer and closer. He had caught their scent and traced them to the foot of the tree. He prowled round and round, looking up hungrily.

The cat and bird were terrified!

Peter was afraid too. Now he knew there really was a hungry wolf and that he must not leave the garden. But he had to help the cat and bird. Suddenly he thought of something. He ran to fetch a rope and scrambled up across the wall into the tree.

Down below, the wolf
prowled faster round the tree.

Peter called to the bird, "Fly round his head."

So the bird flew down just out of reach, and
the wolf swept round and round in excitement.
Soon he began to feel dizzy.

The wolf started to stagger.

Peter made a loop and lowered his rope
round the wolf's tail. Then he quickly pulled
it tight. The wolf snarled and crashed on the
end of the rope.

But he could not escape.

Luckily some hunters were over in the forest. They heard the wolf and rode out into the meadow.

"Over here!" yelled Peter.

Grandfather heard the noise too, and came out of the cottage. He was furious.

But when the hunters told him what Peter had done the old man glowed with pride.

The hunters took charge of the wolf and carried him away.

From that day Peter was much more careful.

BUT THE WOLF WAS NEVER SEEN IN
THE MEADOW AGAIN!

About the illustrator

CLIFF WRIGHT, a prize-winning artist,
began his work on children's books in 1986.
Since then he has written and illustrated
a number of books for various publishers.
He likes to bring his interest in
natural history into his projects.
Cliff is currently involved in a campaign to
save the Canadian rainforest and its bears –
painting cards, posters and books.